Inside Voices at the Girl Aquarium

By Gina Inzunza

Summary: Six teenage girls meet each month at a poetry workshop in New York City. Through writing and sharing their work, the girls deal with issues like peer pressure, family troubles and bullying.

In Memory of Liza Oberg,
1965-2000

Inside Voices at the Girl Aquarium

crowds press as they pass the ocean tank   backlit
glass walls   coral cement   swaying fins of hair   fanning
no bubbles   stingray eyes   pearly dress   no splash

legs jellyfish pulse   torsos slow-mo torpedo twists
arched spines flip behind the hot-

pink treasure chest
a hiding spot

until the shock collars prod them to undulate
undulate   mouths burst open   shoot soundproof
piercing songs to puncture the skylight above

Contents

Lorna   Adela   Lulu   Celeste   Autumn   Tamara

September

Interview Poem

Lorna

Imagine I'm in front of a mic and you're in the audience. Behind me are five other girls. You know one of us, I'm not sure which one. Let's just say it's an event for a good cause. There's a banner above that reads something like, "Save the Girls!" It could mean whatever you want — runaways, anorexia, sexual harassment, teen pregnancy, abuse, the glass ceiling waiting for us at the end of the road, whatever. There's plenty to choose from. Imagine you care about what girls really think. You know that the six of us have spent the last year in a writing workshop, and now we're here to read. It's not a real poetry slam — we're not competing. Well, not against each other, but the world is one big competition, right? So I guess this slam is us vs. the world. Ms. Dee, the poet who ran the workshop, met us at a school in the city on the second Saturday of every month. At each class she'd give us an exercise or assignment. The first time we met was in September, and since most of us didn't know anyone, she told us to pair up with someone and go through a list of sixteen questions. I interviewed Adela, and she interviewed me. We had to write all the answers down and then give them back to each other. Here's all the questions and how I answered them:

1. What is your age? *16*
2. Where do you live? *Teaneck, New Jersey*
3. What is your favorite color? *Baby blue*
4. What is your sign? *Pisces*
5. What is your favorite kind of animal? *Seals*
6. What is a favorite place that you have visited or want to visit? *The Dead Sea*
7. What is a physical activity you like to do? *Swim, dive*
8. What kind of music do you like? *Cool jazz*
9. What is one of your physical traits? *Curly hair*
10. What is one of your personality traits? *Sensitive*
11. What is your favorite food? *Smoked salmon*
12. What is something you like in nature? *Waves*
13. What kind of job or volunteer work do you do? *I teach violin*

14. What kind of job do you want? *Musician*
15. What is your religion, if any? *Jewish*
16. What's something you do to feel better when you're scared? *Turn on all the lights*

Ms. Dee said to take the words and use them to write a poem. We also had to use our first name in the title. So this is how it began, with an interview poem.

Lorna, the Jewish American Pisces

I count 16 seals
performing
in the dead sea
off Coney Island
I teach them violin
they teach me
to dive
like a lost musician

I swim in baby blue
my curly hair relaxes
underwater   sensitive
to sounds I hear cool
jazz bubbling
through the waves
I listen hard
to the inside voices
at the girl aquarium
the muted tapping
on the glass
I memorize woe
the soprano sax quietly
wails

for dinner
I smoke salmon
then follow the river
to Tea-
neck, I shoot
off flares and
turn on all
the flood-
lights just before
sundown

 Adela

I almost didn't come tonight, or to the workshop, either. Who comes to these things, anyway? Freaks, losers. But here I am, so I must be one of them. I guess, so are you. On the first day, Lorna came with Lulu. They're best friends, but Ms. Dee wanted them to interview someone they didn't know. So Lorna asked me. She likes to talk, which helped. I mean, she's from Teaneck, New Jersey, and I'm from Flushing, Queens. I think I've been to New Jersey like two times in my life. Anyway, Lorna made me feel better. She actually seemed interested in my favorite color and what foods I liked. Her handwriting was horrible, though. At least I already knew the answers. So, here's the poem I wrote with them:

Adela, Gone Wild

Sixteen
roaming Flushing
I paint nails   massage feet
I like dark chocolate and Mink
my cat and old movies like *Doctor Zhivago.*
I have thick eyelashes. My clothes are vintage
1970s. I do sit ups for fun   for the day I can swim
at Miami Beach   go clubbing   hip hop all
night. I write to my Dad once a week
in my head. I dance down waterfalls. I hum
to myself when I get the creeps. I lie
about my silver birthday since Scorpios
aren't popular especially
atheist ones. I'm between
guys   very picky
about life
because
life has
rarely
picked
me.

Lulu

It's true what Adela said — Lorna was the one who wanted to come to the poetry workshop. We both like to write, and we even wrote letters to each other this summer when Lorna was at camp. I didn't go anywhere. I was grounded. It was dumb. I got arrested for shoplifting nail polish, and there was other stuff that happened with this guy I liked. Anyway, Ms. Dee is a friend of Lorna's mom. That's how we heard about the workshop. On the first day, she wanted us to help get the group talking. So I asked Celeste to be my partner. She seemed quiet at first, but when she told me she liked to act, that was it. Celeste told me about the time she played Bilbo in *The Hobbit*. I thought that was really cool. I told her my mom was in this group Up With People when she was young. They went around singing to schools. The old videos are hilarious. Anyway, this class was a lot more fun than I expected. What we wrote about was pretty intense, but I guess what I liked about the workshop was seeing everyone get into it. I got into it. So here's what I did with my interview poem.

Up With Lulu

I sing in marigold
I dance in a stretched canvas
I ask monkeys to pose in the nude
  mid-swing
I babysit still life
  bald steamed dumplings
  16 symmetrical orange slices
  in a sweet 'n sour cabbage patch
I wash dishes on a stool and dry them on an easel
I sketch on a menu
I recite the directions from Teaneck to Paris
I come from a Chinese vault, now an adopted Gemini
I speak in artist
to a friendly audience wearing headphones
I cut and paste short people
I pray in Methodist, electric hymnal
up with techno!
I swing and miss
I peddle, I spin
I whirl — stationary
I believe in sunrise
in all its oversaturated shades of pumpkin

 ## Celeste

There's something you should know about me, but it's something I don't like to talk about. It's important, though, because a lot of my poetry wouldn't make much sense unless I told you. So anyway, it's that my father committed suicide a year ago. I actually was the one who found him, in the garage. I've had a hard time dealing with that — I mean, who wouldn't? This class has been something I could hold onto for the last year. It gave me a way to let out all this jumble of stuff I was feeling. The first day I knew it was going to be good because, for a second, I forgot. Lulu and I started talking, and it was so natural. She just handed me my words, the answers to all the questions, and suddenly I began to write.

Celeste On Air

mad about lavender, I shampoo fur
and clean crates at the animal shelter
acting to wagging tails
running lines with the broom
Snowball licks my hand
and we listen to grunge, but if I could
I would do 15 double flips on angel food cake
bounce from cloud to cloud, swoop with seagulls
stretch out my Egyptian neck above Port Washington
and migrate to Aruba. I would use scarves
as wings and whistle at approaching storms
my half-Muslim half-Catholic modesty would morph
into an alias, Amina the flying Aquarius

 Autumn

I guess we all have issues. Mine is depression, which is why I ran away from home. It wasn't for long, but still, enough to change everything. So I think it's been great, the writing, Ms. Dee, the other girls. Something happened to us in this workshop. The poetry shook us up, let us speak about what we couldn't before. Plus I was paired with Tamara, and she is extremely good at shaking people up. Me especially. She notices everything and isn't afraid to ask about what seems off. She doesn't ignore what most people want to sweep under the rug. Now here we are standing in front of a room full of people, some friends, some strangers, about to open up and spill our guts. That would have been my worst fear a year ago, but now I'm actually excited about it—I mean I feel so alive.

Autumn, the Girl, Not the Season

I was born in the Pelham library
with a birthmark on my back
The shape of a mustang. I make films —
stop action with pine trees and folk and flip books
I hike Yellowstone moonscapes
I trudge like a Taurus, a camp counselor
giving out 17 high fives and hugs and big Catholic
warm fuzzies dyed in turquoise
I take communion with sushi
instead of wafers and imagine God
sitting next to me wearing tie dye

Tamara

Let's face it — none of us wanted to come to this thing. For me, it was a teacher who told me about it. I was thinking, no way, but Mr. Ramsey kept on me about it, made it sound like a frickin' Disneyland for girl poets or something. In a way, though, what he said was right. I didn't notice it at first, I mean I'm talking to some white girl about our favorite animals and the mole on her back. But this girl was Autumn, and it wasn't hard to tell in a few minutes, she had some kind of direct connection with God or something. Even though she's had a lot of trouble, she gave off this aura of calm, and it calmed me. For someone whose life is full of chaos, it was exactly what I needed. I never would have admitted that at the time, but it made me want to come back. It was safe there with everyone. And I think that's what was so amazing to me, for once to feel safe. Finally I could say what I had seen, done, lived through. It was okay to be myself and read my poetry.

In Tamara Time

tough feet
walk on coals
broken bottles
run barefoot
in the barrio
dog paddle
to Hawaii
tiptoe the rim
of a volcano
born Baptist
kick gold ashes
for fun

left-handed
with eyes closed
scan mangoes
in Harlem
a cheetah
with a barcode
beep in poet speak
a cashier counting
backwards
16 stars pop
an Aries attracted
to the flames

October

Person Poem

Lulu

The next month we had to write a poem to a person. Ms. Dee gave us different examples of how poets have done this, and one of them was a letter poem. I haven't written many letters, but it was kind of cool to get them when Lorna went to music camp for a month. We decided to take a couple of our letters and turn them into poems. Here's what I wrote to her:

Dear Lorna

How's Blue Lake? How's swimming, boating, hiking?
Do the violins and cellos wear colored T-shirts?
You've probably met a guy named Forest or Trevor—
pale with dark hair, awkward, plays French horn.

I'm grounded. Lots of chores, yelling, silence, SERIOUS
discussions—pretty much on lockdown, except work.
I'm reading everything George Orwell.
The "feels-like" weather is creeping into the 100s —
too hot to sleep, plus the moon has been keeping me
awake/ hostage/ safe. Do you tell spooky stories
to your bunkies? Here's a good one—
    guy and girl doing it in car
    man with hook outside
    scrapes door
    guy opens door, noise gone
    girl is freaked, slam
    they drive off
    get back home
    find bloody hook in door (insert screams)
But you have better ones. Tell them the one about the cook
with the pickled hearts.

Papa Tony's is the same. The bus boys bring me tubs full
of pizza crusts, cigarette butts, beer bottles with chew spit.
I spray it all down, but I can't wash enough to keep
up with demand. Anyway, who eats pizza with a fork?
I bet the food at camp is pretty good—apple butter on pancakes,
chocolate milk galore, and if you serenade the table servers,
they probably bring seconds of bacon. I bet they bring you seconds
of anything. I bet you made First Chair, and the beaming stars,
the Big Dipper even like to listen.

I'm not allowed to see him again, but sometimes, very late
I slip out the sliding door and go barefoot up the backyard
through the Reynolds', the Clarks', the Turners'
to his dark house. I think he's on vacation. The roses look weak,
but they keep me company.

Twelve days before you come home … ugh. When you get back, maybe they'll let me take a ride with you in the Blue Bomb. We can sing with the windows down, drive to Tasty Twist and you can tell me how stupid I was about the hook, and the car, and him.

Miss you…skyfuls.   Love, Luluboo

Lorna

Letters are proof in your hands that somebody actually likes you enough to write something on paper with a pen, and then find an envelope, find a stamp, find the address, find a mailbox, do all this stuff, just to tell you something that's all going to be a week old when you get it. When I got Lulu's letter, I felt bad that she was having a hard time and we couldn't talk, so right away, I wrote her back.

Dear Lulu

Your letter came during the monsoon, during F.O.B.
(foot on bed) time. The ink was blurry, but the stationary
smelled like your cookie candle. I read it 12 times.

I've decided to steal a canoe, paddle back home and pop
your scrubbing bubble hell. My bunkies liked the pickled
hearts, but your stories were scarier — hooks, cars, boys, roses —
STOP! Turn them back into thick air.

I sent you a bookmark that I cut from a strip of leather, trimmed
with fringes, pressed with flower shapes and colored with Sharpies.
Obviously, it won't go with that downer Orwell.

We all take turns being table "hoppers." Mine was Taco Night.
I carried dozens of little bowls of cheese, tomatoes, onions and salsa
to the vultures. I hardly got to eat. Seconds don't exist.

As far as the Big Dipper, he hasn't even showed. Same story …
I made second chair. Round Lake Camp royalty girl, Jank Face, got first.
And, yes, violas wear purple, cellos are yellow, violins fire-engine red.

Camp only has one flush toilet — in the nurse's cabin.
I have pink eye. So does Evan. He has percussion biceps,
auburn hair, a restless tapping foot and the nickname Inwood.

So, I lied to my dad, which was dumb because he'll see me
at the concert. Whatever. I don't want to be in orchestra anymore.
So, probably no more Blue Bomb for me. So, I'm sorry.

But I have decided to steal the aluminum canoe and two paddles.
I'll row from the Mohawk River to the Hudson and pick you up
at the Palisades sometime around Thursday.

I'll be wearing fire-engine red.

Miss you … Milkywayfuls. Love, Lorna

 Autumn

I've been in volleyball since I was eight. Then this summer I broke my ankle and had to have surgery. It still isn't right, and the doctor said I couldn't play anymore. I was one of the setters for the varsity team and really miss it now. I miss knowing exactly how someone else will react in a play, what they're going to do next. I miss winning. I miss hanging out with my friends after practice, especially one in particular.

The Spiker in Slow Motion

diving, the libero digs
      as the ball bumps off
her open wrists

I side-shuffle
   looking through the diamond
     shape of my hands
      I hold up between my thumbs
     flicking on contact
   with the pads of my fingertips
setting the ball back up

      feeding you
        already in the air
           palm cocked behind your ear
              flying close, winding back, arching
                then snapping smack
                  past blockers' outstretched arms

and thunk!
leather whomps
on hi-gloss floor

     Yeeess! we jump
       slap hands pump
    hugging in a bunch
    I hold your shoulder
    your loaded shoulder
    your beautiful, bare shoulder
and yell

I love you!
in your face

and oh

your smile

 # Adela

When I wrote this poem it took like 20 versions to get it where I felt like it was done. The main reason I struggled was because it was about someone I love but don't really understand. I think I was about eight when I started to realized what my aunt did for a living. My mom has MS, so when she wasn't doing well my Aunt Emily would have me come over and hang out at her spa for a day. She told me I was her guinea pig and put weird colors of polish on my nails or gave me a facial with some new mud treatment she'd just gotten. The problem was, her other business kept interrupting us. The phones never stopped, day or night. It was always men calling, and she'd have to leave and go pick up one girl here, and take another girl there. She called them escorts. I didn't know exactly what that meant, but I knew there was something about it I didn't like. In her office, where I'd wait, she had a TV. One time, when she had to leave, I was watching *The Wizard of Oz*, which scared the crap out of me, especially alone.

Happy Endings Day Spa

Auntie Em,
the 14 phones in your Coach bag
frighten me.
Some flip, some slide, some touch
but they all ring
sooner or later.

During our jasmine tea and chit chats —
suddenly, the doorbell ringtone
and you have to answer.

Maybe it's a scarecrow
who wants a Glenda.

Then during the mani-pedi,
you're painting my little toe poppy glitter —
suddenly the hourglass ringtone
and you stop.

It's a tin man who wants
a darling munchkin.

Next time you're in the white cosmetic coat
squeezing tubes of make-up onto a palette
of ruby and petal blush, whisking my cheeks,
war paint, you call it —
suddenly the BAG
blaring a flying-monkey ringtone.

It's another Oz calling,
looking for a wicked witch.
You have them all, north, east, west,
so you drive them in your Toyota crossover
to the Whitestone Palace Motel.

Half a head in sponge rollers
I sit watching TV and the hourglass
drizzle, wondering
if you'll ever have to send
a Dorothy.

Tamara

This summer I liked this guy, Jake, but he was hard to figure out. He'd be all nice to me one day, then the next, it was like he didn't know me, like he couldn't be seen with me. Maybe he had another girl, maybe he didn't want to look like he had a girl at all. But the part that bothered me the most was when we were hanging out together, he'd do little things that hurt, like shoot a rubber band at my leg or twist my arm. He said he was just fooling around, just teasing, but I got the feeling it was no joke.

Rough Play

you press the weight
of your legs down
dig your knees
behind mine
fake slap
bite small marks
on my arm
pinch soft parts
hug me like a boxer
in a squeeze lock

I clench, go stiff
my gut is a pound
of ground chuck

but you got
everything I want
a washboard
a wad of cash
a steel drum

 *Celeste*

I agree with Adela that this was a hard poem to write. Even though we started this in October, I didn't finish my poem until a week ago. I guess sometimes it doesn't come easy and you have to let it sit on the shelf for a while. This fall, we sold our house and moved into an apartment because of money problems, but also I had the feeling that my mom was trying to bury my dad in another way. It was like she needed us to get away from all the reminders, because they hurt so much. Even so, the memories were all we had left — that and his stuff.

Relocated

we moved
in case you're curious
or even can be curious
in case you exist on some "other side" place

Mom sold the house and gave away all your clothes
she asked if we wanted anything first
I kept your flannel coat
Angie kept the navy scarf she made you
Brice kept the Nolan Ryan T-shirt
Mom kept a few things, a tie
    a suit — like a whole nice outfit for some special occasion
later I found your work gloves by the wood pile
I kept those, too

but now there isn't any outdoor work to do
because we're in an apartment, two bedroom
Mom sold other things, the big screen, the tent, your books
she works a lot, she didn't bother with Thanksgiving
instead she took us to a movie
and smuggled candy in her purse

she doesn't ask us about school anymore
don't worry
we all do what we gotta do
it's the only relief, the routine
actually, it was a relief to move
no more garage, no more sudden memories, like gloves
almost, no more you

except sometimes I catch you in the wave
of someone else's hair or a man jogging in your same shuffle
or in a golden baritone laugh behind a door

then I remember there is no place I will ever stumble
into you, no where on Earth is another you
just the missing of you
I glimpse in myself
when I wear your coat

November

Form Poem

Lorna

Writing a form poem sounds super boring, but I found out that you can really be creative with it, especially when the form you choose has an actual shape. Ms. Dee brought in all kinds of examples—poems that looked like animals or cars or even the state of Texas. She also brought Shakespeare sonnets, haikus and this repeating poem called a pantoum. She said we could even make up our own form. I decided to try and do a shape poem about Manhattan and what it's like to visit there. Now that I'm older, I can come into the city and have a pretty good idea of where I'm going, but even a couple years ago I remember being on a field trip and getting all turned around. Then I realized all I had to do was look up, and everything started to make sense.

I ♥ NYC

In
&
out
of the
subway,
disoriented
at the curb—
what end is up?
Is this the way?
Should we cross?
We climb the steps
emerging at the four
corners of the world,
blinking at the neon
daylight of Times Sq.
Electric flames slide
top to bottom, spray-
ing the buildings with
flashes of bright mer-
chandise, Super Icons
blasting off. We stand
there among the Now
& the ever moving In.
Then go wait in line at
Tiffany's where men
with long side curls go
by handing out cards,
"We buy gold. We buy
Gold." Tour bus guys
& the crazy comedy
show guys try to sell
tickets. At the parade
on the step ladder, we
gawk. I bite some of
your pretzel that gets
stuck going down as
Charlie Brown bobs
bigger than the harvest moon. We go
up the marble steps of the Met to see
Van Gogh on his lilac field under the
painted ceiling and get transfixed by
his orange-stubble face. Below in the
shop the tourists gobble up his prints
as light fades on haystacks, and you
show me his sun flowers erupting.

 Adela

When I was little, I was chubby. I guess baby fat is cute, but eventually it got old, the names, grown-ups pinching me. Then when I was 11, I discovered workout videos. I was horrible at first, but I kept doing them. My mom couldn't afford dance lessons, so this was the next best thing. Anyway, after that I stopped eating junk like French fries and chips. The best part was when other girls started asking me how I had lost so much weight. I was like the Weight Watchers rock star for a while, except I didn't use Weight Watchers. I had my own system. The only problem was that it wasn't all that healthy.

Sit Up Chant

The less I eat
      the more firm
Less meat
      more bones
Low carbs
      fat burns
More reps
      flat abs
Five miles
      thin legs
Kick box
      tone butt
South Beach
      skinny jeans
Leg lifts
      tight hips
Ankle weights
      shaped thighs
Low cal
      drop pounds
Saccharin
      size one
Mom nags
      gives in
Eat this
      for a ten
Spit in
      napkins
Grapefruit
      ribs show
Fen-phen
      head rush
Tube fed
      cool bruise

Hair loss
      big talks
Less sense
      more docs
Therapist
      attention
The less I eat
      the more I've got

Tamara

I tried making up my own form for this poem, but it wasn't really working. So I asked Ms. Dee, and she suggested trying a pantoum poem, which repeats each line twice in a certain order. Sometimes it can sound like a song, or if the person in the poem is in trouble, it can show their desperation. My poem is about when I was a little younger and had a problem with cutting myself. My counselor at school found out and helped me with it. He said sometimes it has to do with low self-esteem or even a cry for help. Anyway, I think this pantoum shows how messed up you get when you tell yourself the same bad stories over and over again in your head.

Double Dare

I will if you will and you will if I will
my palms sweat as I cut tiny slivers
slender lines stretch into red shadows
whole parts of me go crazy numb

my palms sweat as I cut tiny slivers
pierced skin, flower bud burns on arm
whole parts of me go crazy numb
no pretty faces here, just move on

pierced skin, flower bud burns on arm
smiling people call, too far gone
no pretty faces here, just move on
friends tattle mad dull whispers

smiling people call, too far gone
I sit in the mess on the bathroom floor
friends tattle mad dull whispers
how do I clean off this rubber maid skin?

I sit in the mess on the bathroom floor
slender lines stretch into red shadows
how do I rip off this rubber maid skin?
I will if you will and you will if I will

 Autumn

I also wanted to try and make up my own form for this poem. It ended up being six lines per stanza, with a rhyming pattern for the last word of each line. I tried to do a certain number of syllables in each line, but that got too hard. It took me forever to get the rhymes right. Some of them still don't match exactly. Ms. Dee calls that "slant rhyme" and says it works because it fits with the idea of my poem, which is about a family getting ready for a party. There's a lot of order in my home. I mean like chores, schedules, do's and don'ts, but no family can run things perfectly all the time. When I was younger, I used to love helping my parents, setting out the china and cloth napkins. Everything was just so and sometimes we'd even take a picture of the table right before all the guests came. It looked like a work of art. But now that I'm older, somehow I've changed. I don't see things the same way anymore.

Dinner Party

Mom ties the duck wings and legs with string
Dad sweeps the driveway with his push broom
Breakfast is toast, cereal and peeled tangerines
I'm assigned to wiping mirrors, dusting the living room
My sisters polish silver, vacuum the hardwood floors
Then we go make our beds, thank God, I can shut the door

She arranges silk orchids in the foyer
He brings up wine, stocks the liquor cabinet
Lunch is grapes, pretzels, a spoonful of peanut butter
They both make their rounds, come to inspect
Crap, I forgot to wipe the leaves on the plants
The house smells like potpourri and a kitchen in France

She whips garlic potatoes, rattles off the errands
He drives, I run in — Taipei Tailors, Roma Bakery
Snack is a free sample of scones and macaroons
My sisters unload the bags, I set the china on doilies
And fold the cloth napkins under three kinds of forks
I imagine them sipping wine, clinking glasses, pulling out corks

She is frantic, goes to dress, "put on" her face
He lights all the candles, tells us to finish up
Dinner is soup from a can, celery, nothing to taste
My sisters and I eat out of paper bowls and cups
If we hurry, we can have lemon sorbet and cannoli
But then it happens, the doorbell rings

He welcomes the guests with the smile of a host
The Bennetts are always early, why are we surprised?
We clean the kitchen and go say hello, what we hate most
She gives them cheek kisses in a cocktail dress, outlined eyes
We go to our rooms, not wanting to listen
To their laughter and talk and how hard they glisten

 Celeste

I did a shape poem about a game I used to love to play. It's amazing how one thing happens and nothing else is ever the same afterwards. Even little things like playing chess — all of a sudden, I can't even look at a board anymore.

After Checkmate

I am anti-   chess and   checkers.
games are   pointless   just more
rules. who   cares who   wins? who
        is keeping   score for
        all games   ever won
        in a single   lifetime?
Guinness,   God? Mil-   ton Bradley?
yes before   it was OK   when I was
little and   you taught   me all about
        strategy   and logic
        but there   isn't any
        real logic   to life, &
anyway   no game is   fun anymore
with you   gone. now I   cannot stand
playing   any games   at all, even

        solitaire.

Lulu

One of the bad things that happened to me this summer involved my old boyfriend, Sam. After this, a lot changed between my parents and me. It was so hard to be grounded, not to be able to talk to Sam. They took away my phone because I had also sent him some pictures of me that I shouldn't have. I couldn't go out except for work. The thing is, he could have visited me there, but he never did. My dad scared Sam, and I know now that he wasn't as into me as I was into him. He moved on, but it took me a lot longer to deal with it. For this form poem, I picked my version of a sonnet because after what happened, my life felt so controlled.

Big Fat Full Moon

Voice like a creamsicle slides through the phone
Funny, polite, faintly bold in his tone
Walking through yards in bare feet and thin clothes
Gravel and grass and the dew on his toes

Stops on my block where the lilacs have burst
Thump thumping heart, as if squeezed, as if cursed
Kneels like a lamb, but he aches like a wolf
Circles the yard, yellow glow on the roof

Stacking the stepping stones under the sill
Carefully climbs, cannot crush the new dill
Tumbles through window, he falls on my bed
Smells of the night and of everything red

Father, he wakes, hears some movement below
He bursts in my room, and all the us turns to no

December

Memory Poem

Celeste

When Ms. Dee talked about doing a memory poem, she gave us kinds of memories to think about, like when you did something no one imagined you doing, or when you saw something that changed you, or you tried something for the first time or had to say goodbye to someone you loved. The idea I liked the best was remembering something magical. Right away, I knew it had to be about acting.

Playing the Hobbit in Fifth Grade

In a mossy spotlight a monologue unfolds
at the rehearsal space in an empty strip mall.

Backstage dwarves in itchy beards sit on a plaid loveseat
or play with their horns, shields and cardboard swords.

Spotlight two, fly the elves tap shoes
in blue twilight, ribbon swirls and dry-ice fog.

Behind a midnight drape clatter plates, cups, plastic food
that shake from the chug of sewing machines.

Spotlight three, Gandalf lets his vocals ring
on cue with the rose flash from his staff.

In back, a buzz saw sculpts a mountain
to a singing dragon, goblins off book.

Spotlight four, Bilbo steps into a golden ring,
no longer me, an ordinary girl.

 Lulu

I picked a memory of when I did something no one would have imagined me ever doing. It wasn't a good thing, though. I almost didn't write about it because it was so humiliating. Maybe my parents couldn't imagine me doing this, but most everyone does something they regret when they're young, especially when you're desperate to find some friends.

Lifted

Brooke and Mia showed me how
they said to start with little things
bracelets and hair ties, so I slipped
an orange soda pop lip balm into my bag
my heart was rattling behind my ribs
we walked past the big walkie-talkie man
arms crossed at the door
but he smiled and said "have a nice day"
when we got around the corner
we ran to Cuppa Java, laughing
our heads off

then Tanya started at our school
her parents just divorced
I asked her if she wanted to go shopping
so we went on Saturday, I told her what to do
but Tanya picked some colored tights
that beeped when we walked out
the man with the headset took us in the back
and called the police
it wasn't fair, I only had blue nail polish
and peace-sign earrings
but the cop said, they added up

he drove us to the station
took our phones and iPods and purses
then called our parents, Tanya's mom
got there first, mine came at night
Dad wouldn't look at me, Mom stared
hard, the sergeant said if I gave 50 hours
of community service then my crime
could be erased from my record
he called it "expunged"
exactly what I wanted
all I was thinking
when my parents
took me home
please, please, please
expunge me

 Autumn

This poem is about what I was feeling when I left home, what was going through my head. People have asked me about why I left, but I've had a hard time explaining. It almost felt like a religious calling, but it sounds stupid when I say it like that. When Ms. Dee told us to write a poem focusing on an emotion, I knew it had to be about the longest night of my life and about this incredible freedom I had, like I had figured out what my life was for, even if it was just for a few hours.

Not Running Away

When I left
it wasn't about leaving.
It was about ahead, toward,
about following North, like someone wise.
I had nothing,
planned nothing.
I didn't run
away from anything or anyone.
There was no running at all.

I drove,
wrote a note,
locked my parents' car,
called my sister on an old pay phone,
told her I might visit at Christmas,
hung up
and walked
on gravel
in a cornfield
behind a gas station.

I walked toward North
not away, not running,
but feeling the good part of running inside.
I thought I had God.

So why take anything else?

It was my calling
at sixteen.
It was the most freedom I'd ever felt.

I had erased behind,
I had no idea of ahead.
There was no running
but that good burning.
There was no away
but what I dropped.

Then a pickup aimed a spotlight
down the rows, slowly passing, pausing.
I hid in the October stalks
flat in the mud
wanting to run
away, away…
My little adult woke up.
My little God broke.

I slept in an abandoned truck
and in the morning
called collect from a Holiday Inn.
Then my parents came
and picked me up.

Tamara

In the city you see a lot of ugly things, the good and the bad get all mixed up. There are people with money dripping off of them and others with nothing at all, begging for food, even water. Living here, you see it all the time, every day until you hardly notice it. For me, I guess it's more that I've learned to ignore it. But on Christmas Eve, I made myself look. And the most important thing I remember about that day was how wind-bite-your-face-off cold it was.

Christmas Eve Day

In a camouflage
army jacket
walking with his arm
out front
a man jangles
coins in
a paper cup
saying nothing
just agitating
shaking like
it's his turn
with the dice
as he hurries up
the ice-caked
Adam Clayton
Powell Jr. Blvd
rattling his change
ready to roll
wild — his dreads
and bearded face
streak, freeze in
an instant on the
window pane
of the shoe store
as he flaps past me
in his bare
feet

 *Adela*

This poem is about the first time I got drunk, about what it physically felt like. I was at a party my cousin had when his parents were out of town. It wasn't a huge party, but I think everyone there got smashed. It was a lot of fun at first, but I hadn't eaten much, and then it hit me all at once. Nothing good happened after that, nothing even remotely fun.

Tipsy Turvy

quick, look up, look out!

I grab the table slant, dunked in swirls
as the balance goes
loose, floating
      like an ice cube

I try a window
      slide open the lungs
      drink in bright oxygen
and cheer to myself —
      do not puke do not puke do not puke
    panic sticks my shirt to my back

I am finished standing up

flop face down
      into the matted rug
      inhaling dander and dust
try to level the ground
fix a position, get up s l o w l y steady the toxic spin
      grab hold of the lopsided wall
all the pictures fall

find the room, find the bed
      aim for the center
      rip out of Tilt-A-Whirl pull
      crash into the mattress
sway with the rocking room
unclench eyes
      stop looking in
      stop everything

in the morning
school children
under broken glass
stare up at me
smiling

Lorna

Our family usually goes to Massachusetts each summer for a vacation. The place where we stay has lots to do and I usually never get bored, even if it rains. But this last summer, I started realizing that the only people who stay there are white and most of the people who work there are black. I also noticed what people spent their money on, what people thought they needed or had to have. I realized I was part of the problem, expecting things without really appreciating any of them.

Time Share

I am blaming
    putt putt golf
the smell of wet towels
people compelled to dress their dogs
    batting cages with twisted soft serve
    charade sounds like wallow, swallow, hollow
dark berries that bleed onto crepes
Triple Letter Scores
vintage flea markets
pastel windsocks
mist in the Berkshires
air fuming with oak n' spruce, oak n' spruce
the brook splashing down past the footbridge
running into the Housatonic
swirling inside, and nerve blocks
opening a new can of tennis balls
illustrations of fish tackle framed above the king-size bed
and myself

for a black woman Grandma's age carrying linen and a vacuum up the
steps to our unit on the fourth floor

January

Dream Poem

 Lulu

When Ms. Dee told us we were going to work on Dream Poems, I thought she was talking about dreams like What-I-Want-To-Do-With-My-Life poems or How-I-Will-Change-the-World poems. But that's not what she meant. She wanted us to use an actual dream we'd had when we were asleep. We didn't have to use the whole dream — bits and pieces of it were okay, too. The dream I wrote about was one of those frustrating dreams where I was trying to write a list, but I didn't have a pen or any paper. So instead, I was trying to remember everything by repeating the stuff over and over again. It was like a game we'd play in the car when I was a kid. Anyway, the weird thing was what the list was for, so I just decided to name the poem that. It's not all a dream. The end is real. It's me waking up.

Tonight I'm Going to My Boyfriend's House to Lose My Virginity, and I'm Bringing...

my Blistex,
my Blistex and two green-tea candles
my Blistex, green-tea candles and a lighter
my Blistex, green-tea candles, a lighter and the Book of Compatible Signs

I'm going to my boyfriend's house tonight and I'm packing
atomic Altoids
atomic Altoids and my inhaler (because of his cat, Boo)
Altoids, my inhaler and juniper essential oil
Altoids, my inhaler, juniper essential oil and condoms

I'm sneaking over to my boyfriend's and he wants me to grab the harmonica
the harmonica and the Valentine's Day card that plays the piña colada
song when you open it
the harmonica, the Valentine's Day card and my latest poem,
the harmonica, the Valentine's Day card, my poem and ME
and he said not to worry, he has condoms

Tonight my boyfriend's parents are gone and I'm taking
my lucky polished stone
my polished stone and a pack of towelettes I stole from the OB/GYN
my polished stone, a pack of towelettes and an extra pair of underwear
my polished stone, towelettes, underwear and *The Princess Diaries* DVD

except I don't really have
a boyfriend
or my virginity
or even a harmonica

just condoms

Lorna

I love those science museums for kids, where you can walk through a huge replica of a human heart and play with "goo yuck" made out of corn starch and green food coloring. I wrote this poem about a museum inside my head, one about my childhood. Have you ever had a dream where you were crying and when you woke up you realized you were really crying in your sleep? I guess childhood doesn't end in a day, but there is a day that comes when you know you'll never be a kid again, and it's kind of hard to let it go.

Dream Museum

I take a tour of my brain along curvy staircases,
peeping out from windows shaped like nostrils
and lenses. Guided groups pet fluorescent flicks,
pull taffy synapses, roll paper cones round and round
fine sugar threads of memories. I climb the rock wall
with Grandma, swing from a palm tree and sip
fresh-squeezed everything.

The exhibits keep revolving, the hallways are soft,
smushed mazes. The carnival music pipes in
with kazoos and accordions, and I twirl so long
in a dancing skirt that I lose my balance and fall
into the pool of noodles, swimming with giant ziti
for water wings.

When I get out, I tiptoe past the rapid eye
movements, lie down on my wet tongue and listen
to myself humming Brahms' Lullaby.

Then comes the ringing in my ears at the final call
for story time and the pitter of little padded feet
parading up the steps to be tucked away, dusting a trail
of talcum powder and cocoa and chalk on the handrails.
Suddenly, at the base of my skull the pituitary gland
lurches into its big production. This sends my butterfly lids
fluttering down into exhaustion and the tear ducts let me out
slowly on a salt water sleep.

Then I'm back on the couch, groggy, in the blank light
and canned laughter of late night TV.

 Celeste

I had this dream three nights in a row. The first night I was scared. The second night I was confused, and the third night I expected it. When I wrote this dream poem, I also decided to end each line with the same word, like some poems that Ms. Dee had read to us. The word was easy to pick because there were so many doors in my dream. After writing this, I noticed the only door that wasn't in this poem was the door I went through when my real nightmare began. But that door still exists by not being there, by avoiding it, day after day. I'm pretending to be a dog, an actor, a normal girl, but mainly what's on my mind is how to escape my mind, even though I know one day I will need to go back through that door and fix myself.

Knock First

I thought I heard the indoor
cat say to the outdoor
dog that she adores
uniformed door-
men, Lassie says she knows a sniffing dog that can smell every bloody door
knob and has a guard dog at the front door
so she can escape out the sliding door
into an express bus or before they see her slip out the side door
and pull off the dog collar, bringing only what she can carry, but behind Door
Number 1 is a seeing-eye dog who only barks at bad mistakes and door
bells, and behind Door
Number 2 is Dor-
a the Explorer, who calls it "la puerta" and takes me door
to door
begging around the city, pounding the pavement, doors
slammed in our faces, then suddenly opportunity knocks
wearing an Italian suit at Door
Number 3, a huge sled dog
who escaped from British Columbia runs out the pet door
while they slaughter the other 100 (a slow year for adventure vacations)
so when one door
shuts, we slide down the hatch, wet fur, past a stage door
as we close the gate
behind us, then Theodore
Roosevelt rides up on his horse and looks up to the 11th floor
of the Plaza Hotel, when Dor-
is Day jumps out the window
and he asks me if I'm next
door to Pandor-
a's box, but I hop in a cab, stick my head out the window
and bark the whole way down to Mexico

 Adela

This dream made me realize I needed to stop reading so many books about vampires. I know I'm not the only one, obviously there's a lot of us out there. I mean it's become a whole new genre, Paranormal Romance. But it's also like a little addiction, so I decided I needed a break, and anyway I had to read *The Crucible* for school. Well, if you've ever read that play, you'll know that it wasn't much of a break — witches, girls running out into the forest, forbidden love. God, it's been going on for centuries, and now it even pops into my dreams. But this time, it was like a news report flashing before me. So this is how it went:

Word from the Face of the Earth

After all the vampires died of AIDS
the world was rid of seduction.
Stakes were packed again with tent poles,
crucifixes hung back up by the spoon collections
and baguettes smeared with an abundance of crushed garlic.
Transylvania Land took in a record annual 10 million
tourists, most of whom gave blood at convenient kiosks.
Across the US heartland, vacant coffins sat in back lots
rotting, and long tattered capes billowed on clotheslines.

But increased rat and nocturnal fowl activity
suggested possible new viruses were brewing.
Werewolves were thought to have retreated
to Bolivian sleeper cells to regroup. A tweet
even rumored Frankenstein and Sasquatch
on the lam, hiding in abandoned resorts
from Iron Mountain to the Catskills.

Worse yet, young girls were inconsolable —
vowing never to marry, and as usual, taking up
cross stitch and witchcraft.

 Autumn

It doesn't matter if you run away for a night or a year—everything changes. And you can never take it back. I didn't expect my parents to look for me. I didn't think it would be a big deal. I mean I'm almost an adult. In a year the plan was that I'd be off in college. But it was a big deal, especially for my mom. Lately, I keep having the same dream. It has something to do with a Shaker village we saw when we were visiting my grandma in Kentucky. I think I ran away because I was trying to figure out what God wanted me to do in this world, but I found out more about what God doesn't want me to do. Maybe it's really simple, like God just wants us to do whatever makes us happy. At least now I know now that's all my parents really want.

80 Maids a-Dancing

After walking all night for 17 years I heard a pounding then chimes drift over
the blue field called Kentucky. Daylight oozed up behind my back. Mud
caked my boots, splattered my jeans. The sun bulb whitewashed my invisibility.
Off the road the sounds were like chopping and a choir singing a hymn I knew.
I caught the word *'tis*, the word *gift* and the word *free*.

I followed the music to a farm called French Hen Acres, to an old meeting house
with lit-up windows where arms and hands flashed. A girl with pigtails and a pit bull
guarded the door. I asked if I could use the bathroom she asked for the password.
Chocolate milk I said, *close enough* she said. The pit bull licked my hand, and the girl
turned the knob, *all the way to the back* she said.

Hundreds of tomato plants twined along the walls into the rafters, beanstalk leaves
rustled from the step dancing of a girl congregation, small to almost grown
moving in a circle. No benches, an open hall, an old metal sign nailed up
said Grand Central. The echoing music came from their voices and rhythm
clapping and wooden heels stomping the floorboards.

Someone handed me a pair of golden glasses then necks looked dabbed with lemon light
shiny dust lifted and the breeze shimmied through dangling crystals. Orange rainbows
bounced off cheeks, moving lips, up-turned eyes. Their patched clothes fluttered, legs
rumbled like kettle drums, voices piped like an organ of piccolos.

I moved around the group near a skinny cow that chewed on straw and watched.
The bathroom was empty but full of daisies in Mason jars near thick porcelain toilets
with high tanks and pull chains. The faucet was a little pump, the soap cakes
hand-pressed with bits of yellow roses. No mirrors, no sound but my own.

When I went back out, the hall was empty. Only the pigtail girl was left, sitting
on a stool milking the cow. *Where did they go?* She said, *who? All the girls,* I said.
You must be tired, she answered and handed me a tin cup of what she had just milked.

I drank and drank and drank the creamiest chocolate milk I'd ever had. I asked her name
and she said, *Mary, silly.* Then I remembered I had seen her before in an old photo
of when my mom was young.

Tamara

I had to do a report for school about Denmark. I read somewhere that the people in Denmark are the happiest people in the world. I could see why. First, it looks so clean, and second, I don't think they have any poor people there, not like they do here. I've hardly been out of New York City, so when I saw the pictures of Denmark, they didn't seem real. I mean, I see tourists here all the time, in big double-decker buses that drive into Harlem. I wonder why, if they're so happy, why would you want leave a perfectly nice place like Denmark and come here? Maybe they want to see what not so perfect is like. I don't know, but ever since I did this report, I keep having this dream about Denmark, like my life would suddenly be good if I could just find a way to get there. Really, I don't even care so much about perfect. I'm just shooting for normal.

Gone to Denmark to Be Happy

I took the A to the AirTrain to JFK.
I wore my fake fur hooded jacket
and put a toothbrush in my backpack
with a cartoon map of Copenhagen.

I dumped out all my C-Town tips
and pocket change at the ticket counter.
The Nordic pilot had a heart
and let me board the Viking plane.

Goodbye to the piss hallways of the projects!
Goodbye to the slow-ass elevator to the 17th floor
in Building 4 of the Grant Houses.
So long to the fast food trash on 125th.

I've gone to find the bronze mermaid
staring at the Baltic Sea, gone to nibble
Havarti cheese, and if the Danes insist,
I'll even taste a bit of dark smoked eel.

Farewell to the mice behind the fridge!
Adios to my neighbor who deals
who collects favors from my mom
for her habit, for his kicks.

Yes, I've left to roam the villages of cobblestone
and glimpse geraniums that dangle out of windows.
Gone to town squares, to markets where hot glass
is blown into shapes, tinted vases and candy bowls.

I've gone to see how happy feels.

There must be magic in that pickled herring
or a wave from the Queen of the North
or a breath of pure Scandinavian air
and salty mist. Who knows?

But I've gone, so gone to Denmark
to hear another language purr and gurgle
and if I squint hard enough
to feel how happy lives.

February

How-To Poem

 Adela

In February, Ms. Dee gave us an assignment I ended up liking the best, a how-to poem. She said it could be about something you really liked to do or were learning to do. It could even be a recipe, but she said to make it for something off-the-wall, like the recipe for Stuffed Happiness Beach Balls or how to make cinnamon toast for the members of Congress. We also could describe something we really wanted to become, like a famous tightrope walker or bean bag chair designer. She suggested we start by writing out step-by-step instructions for whatever it was we were trying to create or do or become. So I picked the subject of Barbie, because all girls eventually figure out who she really is, and sooner or later every girl has to decide if that's who she is, too. I've known a lot Barbies, good and bad, and by seeing so many, I've become an expert on what the best ones do to survive.

How to Be a New Barbie

First, don't take any Ken seriously
and forget about babies — forever.

Realize that, although you only came with a swimsuit and brush,
you have tons of identical twins, and many, many outfits to share.

Cruise with your top down
and pretend to explore lots of interests and career opportunities
in fact, take on multiple personalities
as long as they are the kind that smile —
i.e., Country Singer Barbie, Pharmaceutical Sales Barbie,
Hooters Barbie, Hipster Shopping Barbie or Super Flexible
Gymnastics Barbie.

Avoid Bitch or Butch Barbie
or you'll be bounced out in the next stoop sale.

Understand that some will want to
       dress and undress you
       experiment with your hair
       play out endless scenarios with you
       leave you naked in a box
       or dismember you.

Don't take it personally,
it's just your owner's idea of fun.
This is why you must always

stay on your toes
throw your chest up
and keep your eyes sealed open.

Tamara

What I do best is run. It's what people have needed to be good at ever since there were people. It's why I'm still alive. It's why a lot of us even exist, because we can move fast or our ancestors could. Not everyone is good at it, but where I live, it's a definite advantage. So this is what you need to know if you're a girl in the projects.

How to Run

First, figure out why your feet have to leave the ground.
Do you need to get to somewhere fast or just get away?
Then choose the instructions below that fit best:

Recipe for Running Away

No stretching required, a pair of shoes is good, but not necessary
instead look for seasonal Blow, Weed or Dust, loaded guns
or distilled malt drunks. Then combine
> 2 shots of dread
> 1 pint of adrenalin

Stab quickly, deep into the thigh near your femur. You will stop
feeling pain and move effortlessly. Pump your arms for added speed.
Your body will do the rest, just flavor with instinct when needed.
To check when done, poke yourself, and if you're still breathing, cool
down with a brisk walk home or chat with police. Wait 2 hours
and remove heart from throat, delicately.

Recipe for Running Toward

Defrost something in the horizon —a traffic light, a building,
someone's back you can follow. Keep it in sight as you preheat
the rhythm to 2,000 steps.

> Check the temperature, if stifling, peel the top layer,
> If cold, grease legs with a ¼ cup gel menthol.
> Keep hands loose, arms at 90 degrees, sprinkle
> with desired amount of rain, snow or leaves.

Insert plugs into ears, set music to spice mix, then roll heel to toe
while controlling airflow.

Remove pain as needed—
whip past cramps
until you are a light and fluffy consistency.

Lulu

In the winter I took a drawing class at the community center. I love art, so I decided to write a poem about what the class was like and what inspired me on one particular day. So many famous works of art by men have been inspired by women. In the picture I was drawing, I was inspired by a boy, and I guess by his shoe. I mean, I think a lot of women are inspired by men, but we never see much of that. I like guys, I really like them—the way they look and the sound of their voices and the way they move. I can't help it, and why should I? I think it's natural.

How to Draw the Sneaker of a Cute Guy

take a class where all the students pile
their shoes in the center of the room
and everyone circles the mound with easels

start sketching with a charcoal pencil on newsprint

>   a frayed shoelace
>   a wrinkled boot
>   a heel worn down uneven

latch your eye on the KEDS of the dark-haired boy

blur its shadow into your Nike swoosh

>   blend the rubber toe into your eyelets
>   crosshatch his canvas into your suede

notice on top of the sneaker where he doodled
silver stars, a helicopter and the name KARA
which has four letters like yours

>   so switch them

no one will notice
no one will care
no one at all

Lorna

I've been playing the violin since I was four, but when I was twelve my dad took me to a rock 'n roll school in the city. Since then, I've learned to play the guitar, keyboards, and drums. I have also covered vocals on everything from Prince to Jane's Addiction to the Beastie Boys. The older kids are in House Band. We get to perform at bars in Brooklyn and Manhattan, usually for friends and family on Sunday afternoons, but it's still cool because the bars we play at are pretty well known. There's way more boys than girls, and sometimes the metal guys get a little much when they perform, like when they take off their shirts and swing their long hair around. I used to like one of them, but he dumped me, so I guess I'm a little bitter now. I also started my own band and have been writing a lot of songs. I think that's where poetry has really helped me. I'm usually trying to put words to music, but for once I wrote what music sounds like to me in words.

How to Play Crash Mansion

I. Drums

everything starts with the metronome in your brain
and your chipped sticks held up — clack, clack, clack
paradiddle tom, clicking the hi-hat cymbals,
fast fill, squeezing in ghost notes on the snare, rim shots,
double stroke rolls, bass pedal booms, hair flying
over your face

II. Keyboards

find the tonic — the signature key chopped
from one of the chord recipes, C-F-C-G, blend
augmented intervals as your spider hands pound out
the melodic contours of verse, chorus, bridge
run your fingers up the chromatic scale and land
bouncing on notes

III. Guitar

in combat boots and a homecoming dress, hit
the stage dragging your long plugged tail and gripping
power chords around the stringed neck, pressing frets,
fast picking and plucking, a vibrato wrist feeding
low tones to the woofer, use a hand slide down-up stroke
to send a riff into the crowd

IV. Vocals

sip on a straw in a plastic bottle full of Throat Coat —
slippery elm with licorice — stash it in your gig bag,
take one last diaphragm breath, then strut on stage
in blue-streaked lights, high tops, leopard pants, and jump in
with a glottal attack

 Autumn

I don't like going to therapy. I skip my sessions, pretend to forget them, join a club at school that meets on the same day. I think the problem is I don't want to have a problem. If I keep going, it means I still have a problem, there's still something messed up inside. I actually like the therapist — she's given me ideas that have helped, like writing in a journal and working out more to increase my endorphins. I started kickboxing, and I'm sure I'm doubling my endorphins. She also suggested meditation, which I had read about in a magazine and thought was worth a try. Plus it sounded pretty easy — just breathe and don't think of anything, keep focusing on breathing, and that's it. But I'm miserable at not thinking, I can't stop, not even for five seconds. What's frustrating is that of all my doctor's suggestions, I think this one might actually help the most. I just can't seem to relax enough to relax. So I guess this is an "anti-how-to" poem.

Calling All Karma

if I knew how
to hush
I could deflate
the white noise
in my head
if I knew how
to meditate
I could pad
my skull with
indented foam

if I knew how
to pray
I could serve
my grief
back to God

then my
breath
would
settle

and my
hands
would
steady

and my
mind
would
pause

and all three
would fall
in line
perfectly
like a girl
skipping
down
the
walk

Celeste

People can be really stupid when someone dies. They say things they think will help, but mostly it's horrible, painful crap. So if you ever have to go through any sort of tragedy in your life, I've learned a few tips that can help you deal with all the do-good people who come out of nowhere and try to surround you.

How to Smile When Your Life Really Sucks
(But You Don't Want Anyone to Know How Bad)

beware of super-concerned people
      they're just keeping a tally of all the souls they save
      or want to sleep with someone you know
      or have a remedy to sell

so pretend this person is a hilarious clown
they're a joke, you know that, and any second
they will get a lemon meringue in the face
or trip over their big silly shoes
or hand you one of 20 colored handkerchiefs
so just stretch out their ridiculousness
into a nice little grin and nod
and walk to the nearest bathroom

also, don't be a Debbie Downer —
it's a giveaway, they're onto that (the slumped shoulders
lack of eye contact, piercings, the whole Goth thing)
you're just asking for it, all the sickly questions
    Are you eating enough?
    Would you like to try some of my shea butter hair conditioner?
    Is your mom dating yet?
    What happened to your dad's car?

so instead, be polite and bring up WHATEVER they're into
the Nicks or their reupholstered furniture or chili fries
think of them at the carnival
like you just handed them your ticket to the Shoot the Moon swing ride
smile right through the turnstile
and walk to the nearest bathroom

avoid the corners of rooms, know where the exits are
hold a half-full cup, but never drink
never eat, take antihistamines before you go out, carry baby aspirins
even when the whole crowd is wearing black

and boring holes into your back
turn and react—a party, piñata, streamers, hooray!
      they hand you a present, their hand
      shake it hard and give them a look, a wink
      like you know what's in it
and are so damn thankful
then make a beeline to the bathroom

March

Emotion Poem

Tamara

So this month was a poem about a strong emotion, which wasn't hard to come up with because living in the projects is basically a lot of bad on bad. Behind doors, in the halls, on the elevator, it's people at the bottom with a bunch of other people at the bottom. Sometimes it feels like I'm trying to climb out of a huge pit—except that we're high up, on the seventeenth floor. I want to blame my mom for all this hell we're in, but I try to tell myself it's not her fault.

Not the Apron Kind

I want to wash
your breath and scrub
your words and rinse
your brandy mouth
and feed you what I made
for lunch — a dish called
"empty your glass and
cigarette flush."

I want to hang
your heels behind
the door and wipe
off everything
on you that's false
and all those men
with butterfingers —
they can get
a little chop.

I want to swat away
your ugly talk,
your slurred tongue,
cage your leopard leotards
and sing back all
those lullabies about
a street smart girl
with a pearly smile.

I want to dump
the row of bottles
by the sink and shush
your hoots and hollers,
and squeeze all the sangria
from your eyes and plead
and beg and ask
you to please
bring back
my other mom.

 Autumn

This is a poem to all the people who've tried to tell me how to get rid of my acne. Sometimes complete strangers come up to me with some kind of home remedy. I mean, it really gets old. I guess people like to fix other people's problems. Maybe they think they're easier to solve than their own. They think it's simple, they think I haven't tried anything, everything. Whatever.

Oily

the man with the yellow hands
opened my blemishes with a small razor
and examined, for a fee, my clogs
he dipped a swabbed tongue depressor
in liquid nitrogen (a frozen sparkler)
and rubbed my skin, which fizzed
in tiny explosions
he gave me huge doses of Vitamin A, gelatin pills,
that slowly cracked my lips and the inside
of my nose

and he said remember — never, never touch,
hands off, my face

a wrapped woman from India
in an airport bathroom
told me to apply egg yolks nightly
to smooth out my bumps
the magazines urged —
Open Your Pores! Open Your Pores!
with boiling water in a bowl
just lean over, under towels and melt in the steam
the Mary Kay Lady offered me pink clay
she smudged into a mask
that hardened, so I could move nothing
but my eyes

and she said, remember — never, never touch,
hands off, my face

I am oily, nothing makes it stop
no matter what I avoid
no matter the sun
no matter how hard they scrub
and if I am oily, then so be it —
my oil protects me,
keeps people away who are offended
by my complexion, by complexity

who I want to tell —
never, never touch,
hands off, my face

 Celeste

To help us get started with the emotion poem, Ms. Dee had us do all these crazy exercises, some writing and some more like theater games. We had to take a poem that was about one emotion and read it in a totally different emotion. To show us, Ms. Dee read "Daddy" by Sylvia Plath. First she read it with anger like you would expect, but the second time, she mixed it up and read it like a stand-up comedian. Then she gave me "The Raven" by Edgar Allen Poe, but I had to read it like a nursery rhyme. Everyone got kind of wacky and funny. By the end, we each had an emotion we wanted to use. Then Ms. Dee gave us a bunch of magazines. I got *National Geographic* and *Better Homes and Gardens*, which made a strange combo, but I guess that was the point. We were supposed to pick out words from the magazines and then write a poem using them to fit with our emotion. The problem was, I'd picked a lame emotion, surprise. I mean there's not much to surprise — it just happens and then it's gone. I knew I needed a better emotion, but I couldn't decide on one. It was hard, because at the time it seemed like I didn't have any feelings left in me at all. But when I started to look at the magazine pictures of all those perfect homes and living rooms and china cabinets, I suddenly got so mad. I mean, it looked like the people who live there should be the happiest people on earth, like matching table cloths and napkins could make a family live in bliss. It made me sick, it was such a lie.

An Unusual Pet

My anger still wants to be angry at you
so every morning I take the elephant out on a stampede.
We crash through backyards
blow out pond water
toss metal trash cans on the sidewalk

but no one cares
only the mailman waves.

Inside we smash windows, stemmed crystal,
the beanbag is crunched and leaking pellets,
the sofa collapsed, the books toppled off their shelf.
It's very cramped in the living room,
I lie against her hide when she's asleep
and even dreaming, my anger still wants to be angry at you.

Everyone is careful not to say her name,
to walk around her, edge the wall
like it's normal, but she is not friendly
or gentle, she could crush any of us
which is why elephants wear chains
behind the tents at the circus.

Everyone is careful not to say *my* name
to step around *me*, like it's normal for a girl
to come home early and find the car running
inside a locked garage

which is why my anger still wants to be mad
and ram her head against the steel door.

Lulu

I've always been boy crazy, but this year it was bad. I guess it's like what they say about teenagers and hormones. Anyway, a lot of my emotions starting in March were about a guy in my Spanish class, Benny. Sometimes I think this feeling when you really, really like someone—it's a drug. Something chemical in your brain takes over—you can't sleep, you can't eat, you can't focus on anything at all. And all of a sudden the world is like six times brighter, the colors pop, the smells lift you off the ground, birds chirp in surround sound. For me, this feeling took over my body—I was possessed.

My Spanish Class Crush

Sky is not sky —
it's ozone, soaring azul.

Rojo is not red,
it's rubies and berries

and boy is not boy
anymore.

He's a colt, a cliff
diver, a matador.

Smile is not smile —
but a cascade, a beam,
a magnetic lasso.

Skin is not skin —
it's peach tissue paper,
pressed cotton
and run is not run
anymore.

It's fluid angles,
propellers, rush.

Leaf is not leaf —
it's a señorita's fan.
Hand is not hand —
but mano, some plush landscape
to explore
and eyes are not eyes
anymore.

They're laser and crystal and hazel
all swirled up
and when they fix on mine

I am not a girl—
I'm a dahlia, a gale, la falda
the whirling dress
on a Mexican dancer.

Lorna

I wrote about school and boys, too, but my poem was mainly about a girl who got pregnant and how this group of guys always made fun of her, until she dropped out. Last year they were all about getting her into bed, but after she got pregnant, she was a joke to them. Not just her. They would judge all us girls, making comments when we walked by, nasty. I felt it all day, in the halls, in the back of the class. I wanted to flip them off, I wanted revenge, but that would be suicide, so instead I wrote this poem.

Homework Tonight

Sixth Hour — Spanish
   practice 15 conversational phrases
me llama "Rita," me gusta los charRos
Senora rolls her Rs
they tumble and spin off her tongue —
chaRRRos, cowboys, chaRRRos
my Rs are not round, they drop, they growl

Fifth Hour — American Lit
   read 3 chapters of the Scarlet Letter (an A,
not my grade) her name is Hester, reminds me
of the real Rrita, who left hardly a sophomore,
I see her at the Smile Deli with her baby
   lost in song

Fourth Hour — Biology
   collect 15 samples of bugs, spiders don't count
I found seven of them in the house — a roach,
a fly, a carpenter ant, a pincher, a gnat
RRroach — I cannot squash them
I must put them in zip-locks and freeze them alive

Third Hour — American History
   memorize the first 15 amendments
right to bear arms
right to speedy trial
right to trial by jury
I see the jury, charRos, boys, every day, RRright outside
the bathroom, this is how they grade
(nice) A--, (what a) B----, (already) F----d

Second Hour — Geometry
   study for quiz — Pythagorean Triples
right angles — 3, 4, 5 relationship
15 questions, A squared plus B squared equals C squared
the Egyptians tied 12 knots in a rope equal distance apart
to lay corners in their fields
the right to bare arms, equal distance apart

First Hour — Orchestra
    practice 15 minutes for each piece
RRondo, RReverie, concerRRto
elbow at a Rright angle, ¾ time,
crResendo every 5 measures
remember legato

Zero Hour — Health
    finish STD report
detail the parasites — nits, lice, crabs
taking root, in the field
in less than 3, 4, 5 minutes, no corners are left
and the sentence is in
the jury shoves her into the cold
with a big F across her chest

 # Adela

Once when I was fourteen, I asked my aunt about her business, the one with all the phones. She said it was nothing, all she did was answer calls and tell the men how much per hour. If the escorts wanted to do more, she said that was up to them, and they never told her. Some of the women aren't much older than I am, and some don't speak much English, but we talk sometimes. Most are Asian, mainly Chinese, but there's some Mexican. I'm a mix of both, so they all like me. Anyway, I've learned to keep my mouth shut because my dad got deported, my mom's sick, and Aunt Emily is all we've got. This poem is about one of the escorts I got to know, Juanita. I haven't seen her for a few months, but I wonder about her. Many times, I've tried to imagine what her life has been like, so I wrote this poem from her point of view. I tried to use lines from hand games and jump rope rhymes because it sounds more jarring if it's a girl speaking. Everyone who works for my aunt is an adult, but I think some of them were working the street when they were younger. Juanita said she started when she was fifteen in Mexico City. I know she wanted a better life. That's why she came here. She had this crazy idea that one of the men would actually fall in love and marry her. The sad thing is, I know for sure that hasn't happened, and it probably never will.

The Ropes

All dressed in yellow
with silver buttons down my back,
I'm a Spanish dancer
who did high kicks,
a Spanish dancer
who touched the ground,
a tiny Spanish dancer
split in half —
        the part that asked no questions
        and the part that knows the lies.

I was sitting in a Sugar Maple with Miss Mary Mack
and Miss Lucy and the ghost of babies past.
We all looked down — here was the steeple,
here was the door, then the ugly people. They pointed
by mistake, they thought we kissed the snake.

The first fellow was nice, but then he wanted more,
said it had to go down my Spanish dancer throat.
"I'll kick you right behind Chicago Line,
cut your little ass, catch your tiger
by the toe, and see if you can float."

The second fellow said, "Salute to the captain
bow to the queen, and turn your naked back
to the dirty submarine."

Miss Mary gave me soap, but it didn't really matter.
Miss Lucy gave me dope, but all I needed was a ladder.
Last night and the night before
twenty-four johnnies came knocking at my door.
Last night and the night before
twenty-four johnnies came knocking at my door.

Hell-o operator?
Connect me number 9-1…
yes, no, maybe so.
Ask me no more questions.

Sometimes I wonder why
boys are rotten,
made of dirty cotton.
Boys are rotten,
think girls are handy,
made of sugar candy.
Sometimes I wonder
how many doctors will it take?
      1   2   3   4   5

First comes love.
First comes love.
First comes love —

all dressed in black.

April

Imitation or Found Poem

 Autumn

In April, Ms. Dee wanted us to try writing a poem that imitated another poem. She gave us a bunch of examples to choose from, like "in Just – " by e. e. cummings and "I'm Nobody! Who are you?" by Emily Dickinson. Then we had to write our own poems with the same kinds of line breaks and punctuation and even sounds. It was kind of hard for some of us, me included, so she gave us another choice, a found poem. For this we had to pick out words from something else, like a magazine article or an advertisement, and then write a poem using these words. I did a found poem from people's statuses on Facebook. Did you ever notice that most of what people post online is full of longing? I put this poem together from a bunch of random comments and turned it into a conversation between two people. I wanted it to be a typical one, kind of sad, kind of hopeful — the stuff we keep saying to each other and ourselves over and over.

Statuses

saturday! woohoo! burger time!!

      hey, remember that hookah place we went to?

it closed : (

      where should I go for the next chapter of my life?
      this working thing, it sucks

the smell of failure is French toast
gone bad

      wuv you

jealousy is a good form of motivation

      i found onions in my coffee

seriouzzly,
I missed your face last night

      the poconos await!

this better happen

Lulu

I like to babysit because it's cool the way little kids don't hold back. They tell you exactly how they feel. Sometimes you know just by looking at their faces. I found my poem from something my little cousin, Carly, told me. I usually babysit her once a week. She likes books a lot and knows how to read a couple words. Before bedtime I always have to read her a story, and afterwards I ask her to try to read me one. She usually picks a book she's memorized, one of her favorites, like *Goodnight Moon*, but one night she grabbed this big book of modern art off the coffee table and started "reading" to me. I was amazed at her imagination and what she saw in the pictures, so when she was asleep, I wrote down everything I could remember that she said.

Babysitting Carly, Age 4, Who Reads to Me from the Coffee Table Art Book

Parrots are whooshing over people's heads
They close their eyes
Because it's raining feathers
Wet rainy feathers keep falling and parrots
Are flying low so everyone is ducking
And covering their heads
And the feathers start turning into flowers and petals
Pouring down in the rain
In the thunders, in the showers
People have drops and petals and feathers
Running down their faces
And they shut their eyes tight
So it doesn't burn
So nothing can get in

Lorna

I did an imitation poem from one by William Carlos William called "This Is Just to Say." It's about a man who asks his wife to forgive him because he ate the plums she was saving for breakfast. But I think he's saying something else to her, wanting something forbidden, maybe because he's married. My poem is about a girl who is writing to her big brother about what she found when she was using his computer. It's not about my brother, since he's only nine. I hate to think about it, but I guess one day it'll probably happen. I think most guys these days go online sooner or later to watch porn. A couple different times boys I liked wanted me to watch it with them. The first time I saw it, I felt like throwing up. The worst part was, once you see it, you can't erase it from your mind.

This Is Impossible To Say

I have deleted
the sites
that were on
your favorites

and which
you were probably
hiding
for after bedtime

scrub me
they were sick
so raw
and so cold

 Celeste

In the first version of my found poem, I used words from my biology textbook, but when it was done, I felt like something was missing. Then I looked at my notebook from class to get other ideas. The notes were a little random because my mind wandered whenever the teacher talked too much, so I would add little comments to myself. During that month, a lot was in the news about protests in Muslim countries, and since my dad's family is from Egypt, I was thinking about the people there and all the uprisings. In science class, I would play with the words the teacher was saying and try to relate it to all that was on my mind. What I came up with was a found poem just from my notes, both from what the teacher was saying and from what I added in the margins.

My Biology Notes Based on True-Life Events

Matter = Anything
that takes up space and has mass

but does anything matter at Mass?

matter exists in many diverse forms
(rocks, metals, oils, gases and humans)

people jam the streets
a mass of humans with rocks, metal pipes, and fuming gases
wanting oil or money from oil

matter is made up of elements,
which can't be broken down by chemical reactions

honking and yelling below
diverse reactions, all because a street vendor
questions a simple matter

92 elements occur in nature
(like gold, copper, carbon and oxygen)

THEN LIGHTS HIMSELF ON FIRE!!

fire needs oxygen

siren screams, hysteria, glass breaking

to burn

shouts, freedom blurs into chaos

about 25 natural elements
are known to be essential to life

to grow, to love, to belong, to express

just 4 make up 96 percent of living matter —
nitrogen, oxygen, hydrogen and carbon

the remains, black smoke, ash, coal, soot,
diamonds, carbon dating diamonds

a compound consists of 2 or more different elements
combined in a fixed ratio

holed up in a compound
the leader waits with guns
reworking his status

for example, sodium (a metal)
and pure chlorine (a poisonous gas)
form the edible compound (table salt)

tear gas is shot into the crowd

another compound, consists of hydrogen and oxygen
in a 2-to-1 ratio

they pour water on the man

all organisms are made up mostly of water

he lives for several hours
in agony

life on Earth began in water
and evolved there for 3 billion years
before spreading onto land

I hold mass inside myself
a sprinkling of candles, taste of burgundy and sourdough

3/4s of the Earth's surface
is submerged in water

then comes chanting

as astronomers study newly discovered planets orbiting stars
they hope to find evidence of water
on these far-off celestial bodies

I take up space, take up space, take up space

I matter

Tamara

I did an imitation, and the poem I picked was by Robert Creeley, called "I Know a Man." I liked how he uses simple words but they still hit me with that desperate feeling. I see it in my neighborhood a lot, on the street, the bus, when I'm working at the grocery store. Mostly poor people shop there with food stamps. You learn a lot about people when you see what they buy week after week. And the people who don't have food stamps — a lot of immigrants — I see what they decide to buy and not buy. There's the people who know exactly how much money is in their wallet and others who spend their last dollar like it is nothing. Eggs are popular, they're cheap, same with rice. People will give us tips sometimes, leftover change. My friend and I joke about what we're going to do with the tips, but when I think about it, I could just ... I don't know. It sucks to be poor, it really sucks.

I Know a Girl

As I sd to my
friend, because I am
always talking, — Gwen, I

sd, which was not her
name, the projects sur-
round us, what

can we do against
them, or else, should we &
why not, take a goddamn big Prada

bag, she sd, for
christ's sake, look
out where yr putting
the eggs.

 Adela

I found my poem in the Queens phone book at Happy Endings. My aunt has an ad in it, under Day Spas, and also in one of the biggest sections, Escorts. I wonder if other girls ever notice these ads and what they think about them. I wonder what women think about them, too. I already know what men think about them — maybe not all men, but enough. The other thing that's really disturbing is that most of the ads are for escorts who are Asian, and they all mention fast delivery, like they're talking about fried rice and egg rolls.

The Queens Escorts

Fast & reliable
We're there when you need us
We welcome all requests
We make your dreams come true
Magical moments, 24-hour service
Ultimate fun time guaranteed

Discreet billing
30-minute delivery!

Prompt & private
Happy Hour specials
Multi-hour rate specials
We specialize in corporate & bachelor parties
Two-girl specials

All major credit cards
30-minute delivery!

Party girls available
Playful, cute, & enjoyable
Oriental flower, oriental dream
Best girls, best rates
Oriental party girls

Out calls only
30-minute delivery!

Prompt, Asian roses, Asian pleasure club
Asian paradise, Asian skin club
NY Asian honey, Asian babe
Top-class Asian girls
Asian sweet waiting to pamper you
Asian joy, new Asian hot kiss
Exotic Asian hotties

VIP treatment for a discerning gentleman
30-minute delivery!

May

Empowerment Poem

 *Celeste*

Back in the spring, something changed for me. It was like when you've been really sick, the worst you've ever felt, and all you can do is curl up in bed and sleep, and no matter what you try, nothing seems to help. Then it happens. One day you wake up, and you feel like eating an orange or reading a magazine or just getting out of bed. It's almost like starting over. Somehow through all the misery, you are given something new, a different way to see.

Grief Cleaning

I climbed out of the heap today
neatly folded my crazy quilt
and straightened up my vertebrae.

I sorted all the lights and darks and grays
bagged up sheets of papered guilt
and climbed out of the heap today.

I fed my bones fresh calcium and rays,
watered every limb threatening to wilt
and straightened up my vertebrae.

I scrubbed my skin with sea salt paste
combed through tangles, brushed off silt
and climbed out of the heap today.

I squared my chin and lifted up the shades
righted frames from all their tilts
and straightened up my vertebrae.

I filled my lungs again, turned on a gaze
restoring the body my parents built
when I climbed out of the heap today
and straightened tall my vertebrae.

 Lulu

This assignment sounded super Oprah to me. I mean, empowerment is usually a word associated with people who have nothing to do with power. Think about it— most CEOs probably don't write a lot of empowerment poems. But Ms. Dee said we were at the point in the workshop where we needed to raise our voices, to make a big noise. Her instructions were to take an idea or feeling and crank it up ten decibels, to write with a "passionate sway." And she gave us permission to lay it on thick and go over the top. So I decided to write about how spring makes me feel. It also helps that May is my favorite month, partly because of my birthday and partly because it's finally full-out spring. I start to work in our garden then, which makes me feel connected to life (and sounds super corny), but like I'm here for a reason, or a million reasons, none of which are important to know at that particular moment.

Birthday

ripe as a lilac
a sudden quiet, then a bird's trill
a flash of heat, racing squirrels
the time of my birth hops on

dripping dogwood, redbud,
honey combs of crabapple blooms
a ginger gust shakes
fingernail petals onto wet dirt
fill an enormous breath

I grab dried nettle and ragweed
yank loose albino roots
clutch and claw away debris
grasp clods, churn the worms
dirt cakes grow on my knees

sprouts stretch toward shining threads
I plant all my worth, I plant pumpkin,
sunflower, corn, handfuls
of magic beans

sprinkle rows, stems shoot up
racing like sap runs and complete
as rabbits who litter the lawn
munching, munching green

 # Adela

When we met in our class, the first thing we did was to read our poems for the last assignment and talk about them. We would say what lines we liked or if something confused us. It really helped me to hear what the other girls thought about my poems. It made me a better writer. And it made me feel less alone. I remember when I heard Lorna's first poem from the interview. She had a line about a girl aquarium, and it kind of hit me. I asked her about it, and she said it was how girls always seem to be on display, but the world doesn't really want to hear what we think or feel. I totally get that. When a girl grows up in the city without a father or brother, she has to figure out pretty quickly how to stand up for herself. She learns early on not to trust anyone, especially someone with a penis. She carries anger, she feels pushed into a corner by guys and their rules and what they want. She feels talked down to, she feels threatened, she feels like a thing, she feels used, over and over again. I know there must be good men somewhere. I've read about some, seen some in the movies, had a couple good male teachers. I know women aren't perfect, either. But sometimes I wish we could have a try, just once, and be the ones in control.

The Girl Manifesto or My Science Project to Fix the World

Wake up plastic-faced sisters!
The power's off, you're free!
Move unplugged, away from the blank screen!
Break out of the Girl Aquarium!
Leave your Stepford Prep and let your "inside voices" out!
Find the exit
Escape from your strung-out boyfriend
Your job at the salon, sweeping hair
Your class on the history of men, mankind, male-bonding
Kick off your stilettos, *run!*
Hurry, down to the bonfire, throw in your acrylics
Douse the Versace handbags with gasoline
Burn someone else's regret
Toss in all the frilly thongs
Tie string bikinis around your biceps
Unclutch your grande cups, and make a fist
Light the American Apparel billboard! Resist!!

This is the Year, the Century, the Millennium, of the Girl
And these are our demands
            We speak for ourselves
            We will not be beaten, bound or sold
            We will not be treated as objects
            We demand to learn
            We will not be second to boys
            We will be heard!

If not, we will organize!
Stage sit-ins at MTV
Desert the sidelines, throw all our Teen Vogues in the blaze
Boycott booty calls
Picket Victoria's Secret
Not play dumb, not flinch, not give it up

And so what if they call us bitch?
Or play grab ass, catcall, insult,
Yell remarks about our body parts?
So what if they stalk, push, smack?

Or stare?
Try to get their way,
Or have their fun, force themselves on us?
So what?

Because this time is different
This time we'll make a secret pact, and from here on out,
We'll bottle up gobs of the sperm they love to spout,
And store it in every deep freezer on the planet

And when we want a baby, we'll pick from a catalogue
Then have a procedure done
And from then on
We'll never ever ever
Have to have
a son.

Lorna

Try this at home the next time you're watching television. Count how many seconds before something demeaning or degrading comes on about anyone female. My highest number so far is forty-six seconds. Even cartoon girl chipmunks have to be sexy now. Ugh. But I'm giving up the whole thing. It's too depressing. I mean, I'm giving up TV completely. Maybe I should give up magazines and movies and the Internet, too. It's everywhere. I've always wondered what it was like during World War II, when most of the men were gone and busy with the war, and women were doing everything else — working in factories, building airplanes, driving trucks. Where did those women go? Did they just evaporate after the war? I know there was a women's movement, but that was like twenty or thirty years later. Of course, a lot has changed for women, and this country is better than a lot of others, but it seems like there's still one big sacred rule that will never go away. Above all else, you must always be attractive and forever give guys the lead.

Conjuring Rosie the Riveter

When I grow up I promise to
    wear heels whenever possible
    always put makeup on before I go out
    find great joy in shopping
    judge women by what they wear
    try every diet but indulge when I hit my ideal weight
    giggle at all men's jokes
    hate science, except when it has to do with a spa.

I cross my heart and hope to die that I will
    own matching handbags and shoes for every day of the month
    tune out the news unless it has to do with celebrities or fashion
    get my nails done weekly
    use cleavage to get men to do the things I can't do in heels
    never go behind the camera
    spend a small fortune on lingerie
    talk about the failed relationships of women I don't like
    ignore politics.

I pinky swear to
    exercise in tight shorts
    spend an hour a day doing my hair
    dwell on the flaws of other women
    use computers only for social networking, online shopping &
    celebrity stalking
    not invent anything
    like sports when I can cheer in a cute outfit
    only read steamy romances
    hate feminists.

On my honor I pledge to
    be religious about sculpted eyebrows and Brazilian waxing
    wish, wish, wish for an enormous engagement ring
    live for makeover shows
    never discover anything
    spend my free time in trendy cafes and boutiques
    hate math, unless it's a sale discount
    and when I turn 18, I vow to become
    the woman America expects me to be!
    Amen.

So until then, lay off
let me play my Fender guitar with the amp up
bang my head against the wall
and sing my new anthem, called
"America, Find Someone Else to Screw."

Tamara

Ever since I can remember, I've liked words—listening to them, reading them, playing with them. I would make up songs, raps, stories. Learning to write was like winning a prize, like when my grandma won a TV at bingo. A year later, my mom was drunk and knocked it over. She was always breaking something, but when I started writing, that was a prize no one could break. I figured out pretty quickly that everyone I knew thought it was weird. Sometimes I think I must have been switched at birth. The people around me didn't read. And poetry—forget about it, I never mentioned that to anyone. My most secret wish has always been to go to school to study poetry. I don't even know if you can do that, but if you could, there's a million reasons why I couldn't. I still like to dream about it, though. Some little college with ivy and old stone buildings and professors with English accents and a library full of books and reading and reading and talking about poems with other people who like poetry, long discussions. And then writing as much as I wanted, never hiding it, maybe even sometimes reading it out loud at a coffee shop or something. That to me is heaven, my exact version of it. So I guess this workshop—it's been like a miracle.

Fire-Breathing Words

my first word was "hot"
I mashed up strange lines from nursery rhymes
about a quick Jack and a candlestick
Daddy called it baby rap
I begged grown-ups to read to me
until Mom dumped Mother Goose
down the garbage chute
but I had memorized every line

I learned to write
collecting words in my Elmo notebook
       like pot
       and little
       red hots
that turned my cinnamon tongue
into lighted butane, my first Valentine
when I was six, the same night Daddy
got shot outside OTB
and I felt the sound of my mom's
unquenchable thirst

at recess, the first song I learned was "Survivor"
by Destiny's Child, I lit up
the spelling bee each year
in second grade I won with "semantics"
my first book was *Pocahontas*
I tried painting my face
I slept with a pocket dictionary
to put words in my mouth

in high school, we read Maya Angelou
and from then on, I had her in my bag
the first poem I memorized was "Ego Tripping"
by Nikki Giovanni who released
a female omnipotence over my head
then I wrote my first verse
called "Freakin' Caliente"
and got a new lab partner, Langston Hughes

I haunted stacks, bargained with Walt Whitman
selling books on the sidewalk
I moved with iambic feet, in a trance
a hip-hop skip, Gwendolyn Brooks and me
sat on the stoop, too cool to jump rope
faces blended into an inner dialogue
blues broke out into spoken word
I sketched hymns with bent sounds
outlined in Aretha vowels

if it hurt too much, I hated in Eminem superlatives
or drank shrinking potion with e. e. cummings
when ma's boyfriend yelled
Emily hid with me under the bed
and if a boy tried to get fresh
Queen Latifah had my back

at my first open mic
my beat bumped so hard inside
my mouth had to run to catch up
run mouth run
see this black Jane bust it up
exhaling meter in jalapeno
throwing rhyme into flames
igniting action verbs
and I fumed and I huffed and I blew
until the TNT in my chest
went off
in Technicolor sparks

 Autumn

I have twin sisters who are in the sixth grade. Sometimes they can be little bossy and fuss about what we watch on TV or borrow my earrings without asking, but mostly they're cool. Actually, I think they're kind of amazing in a lot of ways. First, they have that psychic twin thing going on. But they also have it with me, so it feels like I'm an honorary twin. Like they know what I'm going to say or even what I'm thinking. Maybe that's just a sister thing. Anyway, the second is, they do good stuff — automatically. I don't mean like cleaning their room, they're not so good at that. I mean they have this way of knowing how to help and being fearless at the same time. Like once they saw these teenage boys tie a can to a cat's tail, and they took the fire extinguishers from our kitchen and fireplace and told the boys to stop hurting the cat or they would spray. I mean that took guts. So when Ms. Dee asked us to write a poem about empowerment, I thought about them. In this poem, it sounds like I'm only talking about one, but it's really both, or maybe it's all little sisters everywhere. I like to think so.

The Supernova Powers of My Sister

her jokes make a dying man giggle
I've seen her paperclip a marriage
back together, cough so hard
chain smokers crush their cigarettes
she can pull splinters from a moth
hear a whisper from Bangladesh
and translate it into sign language

she's raised enough white pines
to cut New York's carbon footprint
to a toe, thunderstorms stop grumbling
when she plays her ukulele, her watch
is set to beep when migrating geese pass
overhead, she grew a rare Ghost
Orchid in a milk carton for Mother's Day
and the pollen cured a deadly bee disease

her sidewalk chalk drawings of the Appalachians
were so accurate, a park ranger gave tours
and her pinholes in the night sky made
the Archer constellation morph into a dot-to-dot
girl scout holding up a three-finger pledge

I warn my sister about what's ahead
but right now, she's invincible, cheerful
even on hot-mess days when I want to sink
into the ocean, the river, the pool, the tub
my sister pulls me back up to the surface
and gives me a reason to breathe

June

Group Poem

 *Adela*

For our last assignment we had to work on a poem together. As homework, everyone had to write a few lines describing themselves, but only using similes, because Ms. Dee said we use the word "like" a lot, so we might as well try using it in a poem. She had a rule, though, that we had to compare ourselves to something in science. We could also write lines about who we were not. Each line had to be written on one page, in big letters. When we had our last meeting, we took all the papers and taped them up on the board. We read them out loud, rearranged them, took some off, argued, laughed, and ended up realizing it wasn't a poem just about us. It was about all girls our age.

In the Land of the Teenage Girl

she's not splits
she's not low-cut or high kicks
she's not a ShakeItShakeItShakeIt

no, she's like a photon blur
like the head rush in a cyclotron
like the yank of rising tide

but she's not a prancing pony
she does a quantum leap in stride

she's not an extended eyelash
not a candy-apple toenail
not a belly button stud

no, she's like a snowflake fractal
like fire coral with stinging tentacles
like carpet shock

but she's not a pouting lip
she measures atomic weight on the spot

she's not a mannequin posing in the window
she's not rose petals tossed from a basket
she's not the April swimsuit issue

no, she like the high beam on a quasar
like the speed of radio waves from cockpit to control tower
like the temperature nitrogen wants to freeze

she's not made of hoopskirt cake
her hair isn't peanut butter curls
her dimples aren't ginger cloves

no, she's like a volcano in a bottle
like mixing vinegar and bicarbonate
like a new place on the periodic table
like the element of surprise

but she's not the flavor of the day
she feeds herself on how to thrive

she's not hips swinging side to side
she's not a trophy encased
she's not a little woman or a big girl

no, she's like the green of photosynthesis
like a jet stream beginning to expand
like the first hour after the Big Bang

but she's not a notch on a belt
she's the ultimate hero
Super Keeper of the Human Race
quietly holding all generations
inside her small, infinite space

Acknowledgments

"Word from the Face of the Earth" was originally published in *Boog City*. "Grief Cleaning" and "Birthday" were first published online in *em:me magazine*.

Much appreciation goes to poet Joanna Fuhrman for her invaluable advice, suggestions, and quick encouragement through the many drafts of this book. Thanks also to the participants of Joanna's poetry workshops for their helpful feedback, including Lauren Russell, who also provided meticulous copy editing skills. A huge shout out to Marcus Yi, who helped bring the "Girl Aquarium" to life as artistic director for theatrical performances and videos. Special recognition goes to the actors who were photographed for this book and also enacted numerous poems for the website—Esther Chen (Adela), Katya Collazo (Celeste), Danielle Ma (Lulu), Melanie Siegel (Lorna), Mirirai Sithole (Tamara), and Kyra Sturken (Autumn). Previous actors who also helped in early performances of the play and videos include Angela Collard, Danielle Geeslin, Lotus Huynh, Betty Kaplan, Maxine Magallanez, Erika Meller, and Ingrid Running. Also in these ranks were my three daughters, Teal, Elysee and Miranda Inzunza, who gave me great doses of support, honest feedback and inspiration throughout this long process. Thanks also to Stephen Holt for being a great sounding board and to David Salley who gave me the push to start this whole project. Much gratitude goes to my biggest fans and loving parents, James and Gloria Pocock. Most of all, none of this would have been possible without the support of my husband, Victor Inzunza, who helped in more ways than I could ever count.